To The Reed Gang —
Alexis, Gage, Wesley & Ace
Merry Christmas Bed Time Story
By Great Grandpa Miller
Christmas 2012

Published in Texas by Harbor House Publishing
ISBN 978-0-557-17907-7

Additional Copies:
Rockport Birding & Kayak Adventures
(877) 892 4737
tmoore@Rockport Adventures.com
or
www.TheLobstickPrince.com

Third Edition

In memory of my dad;
Capt. Tom Moore

In 1978 when there were only 72 Whooping Cranes remaining, a special young Whooping Crane came into the world. His family fed him frogs, bugs, snakes, and other delicious Whooper snacks. They taught him to fly when he was only 3 months old.

Then one chilly day in October he followed as his parents took flight and flew higher and further than he had ever flown before. The strong north wind continued to help the family on their journey south. Every night they would stop and rest, standing in shallow water so that coyotes could not catch them.

As the weather turned warmer and the wind blew from the south making it harder to fly, his family finally stopped to rest. Where they landed there was a great river and plenty of food. Many other birds also stopped here to feed and rest.

When the cold north wind started to blow again, they took off and continued their long trip. Then one day the young crane looked ahead and saw that the trees and grasses below ended and all he could see was water. He was very glad when his parents started to fly in circles and landed in the marsh that looked a lot like the place he had left weeks before.

The weather was warm and there were yummy Carolina Wolfberries everywhere. As he and his family walked through the marsh plucking the red berries from the bushes they would come to small ponds that were full of delicious blue crabs. His parents taught him how to stalk and catch the crabs so they would not grab his beak with their pinchers.

As the weather turned colder there were fewer and fewer berries to eat so the family spent more time in the shallow ponds catching and eating the Blue Crabs. Sometimes the parents would dig into holes around the pond and find Fiddler Crabs. The Fiddlers were easier to catch but were not as big and tasty. He also found snakes and rats in the marsh, these were scrumptious and fun to catch but Blue Crab was what he liked best.

The weather turned warm and all of the grass and bushes in the marsh turned a lush green color. In early April the wind blew very strong from the southeast. His mom and dad had been bowing their heads and then jumping into the air together flapping their wings. It looked like fun and sometimes he would join in. It made him feel good. The young crane started to notice other families of cranes flying high overhead. One morning his parents took off toward the north and he followed along wondering when they would stop.

When they reached Canada and the marsh they had left in the fall, his parents would run at him to make him go away. It hurt his feelings but he knew it was best so he searched the marsh for other young cranes to join. He found a group of 4 young cranes and they formed a "cohort" and would all move around the marsh to feed. As a group there was always someone looking around to be sure there were no Lynx or Wolves stalking them.

For the next 2 years, the special young crane would lead the cohort south in the fall to Texas to stay warm and eat Blue Crabs near Aransas Bay. Each spring they would take off for Wood Buffalo National Park in Canada.

In the spring of 1981 our young crane took notice of one of the female cranes in the cohort. He would bow his head and leap into the air and they would do the dance that he learned from his parents. The two cranes searched the marsh for a territory of their own and settled in an area near Lobstick Creek just outside of the Park and spent the summer together feeding in the ponds and creeks.

When they returned to Aransas in the fall they found a long strip of marshland located next to the Intracoastal Waterway. There were many boats coming and going but there were also plenty of crabs and wolfberries so they decided to make this area their winter territory. Every day a large pink boat would come by with people who would take their picture. The captain driving the boat would tell the other people all about them, where they lived in the summer and how they would fly back and forth each year. The Captain called them the "Lobstick Pair" and they could tell the people cared about them.

Most wild Whooping Cranes live to 15 to 20 years. The Lobstick male lived over 30 years. Since the Lobsticks were seen every day by so many people, they became the world's most famous wild Whooping Cranes. As Whooping Crane "Royalty" they helped create more awareness of the problems the rare birds face and inspired more people to do things to help them.

One year upon their return to Texas, they found that the people had placed blocks along the peninsula to make sure that the land would not erode so they would always have a territory on the waterway to raise their chicks.

Most Whooping Crane chicks do not survive, but the Lobsticks were able to raise a chick most every year and some years they raised two chicks which is very rare.

In 2004 the Lobsticks hatched a male chick and brought him to Aransas. He spent the winter feeding in the marsh as usual. Late in the spring as the weather got warmer a Cottonmouth snake struck the young bird on the neck. The courageous bird laid down in the marsh as his neck and head swelled to the size of a basketball. The Lobstick parents stayed with him in the same spot for 3 days as the poisonous venom wore off.

On the 4th day he was able to stand but barely able to hold up his head. The family moved around their territory while the parents continued to gorge on Blue Crabs preparing for the long journey to their Canadian nesting grounds. The dedicated parents stayed close to the wounded juvenile and fed him small pieces of crab when he would eat. His large head began to return to normal size as the poison wore off and he was able to break up the crabs his family caught for him to eat. About 2 weeks after the Lobsticks usually leave for Canada the recovering whooper was finally able to find a crab, catch it, and eat it. When the parents saw this the urge to migrate overcame the urge to raise their young and they left for Canada on the strong southeast wind.

The young bird continued to get better and as the swelling went down a large scar appeared on his neck below his head. This prompted the Captain of the Skimmer, which was the new boat taking people to see the magnificent cranes, to call him Scarbaby, The Lobstick Prince.

The Lobstick Prince stayed in Texas that summer and joined a cohort of 2 other sub-adult whoopers when the flock returned in the fall. He and his cohort moved between territories that allowed the people to see him and hear his story. The following spring the Lobstick Prince convinced the other birds in the cohort to stay in Aransas with him for the summer.

Throughout the summer the three cranes moved around the Refuge feeding on crabs, snakes and other marsh critters. Without the rest of the flock at Aransas the young cranes could go anywhere and not be chased away by other birds the way they were in the winter. Life was good.

As the first few cold fronts arrived in the fall The Lobstick Prince and his cohort began to notice other whooping cranes arriving and re-establishing their territories throughout the marsh. Pretty soon there were pairs of cranes in every available territory and The Lobstick Prince and his friends found an area along the Intracoastal Waterway where the adult cranes would not bother them just as his parents had so many years ago.

Over the winter Scarbaby and the female of the cohort became close and as spring approached they began to become a pair. They would leave the other male bird of the cohort behind and began to do the beautiful mating dance together. As cranes mature and begin to pair up the urge to migrate to the mating grounds becomes very strong so Scarbaby and his new mate took off for Canada to nest.

In the fall they returned to Aransas and found an area along the Gulf Intracoastal Waterway which they declared with loud whoops as their territory just as his parents had so many years ago. In fact, Scarbaby's territory was only a few miles away from his Lobstick parents. The other male bird in the cohort had to find a new territory and a mate of his own. The Lobstick Prince and his mate returned to Wood Buffalo National Park in Canada again in the spring. It will typically take a young pair of cranes 3 or 4 years to successfully raise a chick so they diligently tried to nest again.

When they returned to Aransas in the fall of 2008 a severe drought had eliminated all of the fresh water that usually flows from the Guadalupe River into the marshes of Aransas. This was a very hard year for the Lobstick Prince and all of the other cranes at Aransas. When humans use the fresh water they need and there is no rain, there is not enough water for the animals of the bays and marshlands. Blue Crabs do not do as well when the marshes become too salty. High tides from Hurricane Ike and the lack of rain made it impossible for the Carolina Wolfberries to grow and the blue crabs that the whoopers need so badly had virtually disappeared.

With none of their favorite foods available the Cranes had to find other things to eat. They ate Fiddler Crabs from the marsh and went into the oak forests of Aransas to eat acorns. Whooping cranes live in the marsh to stay away from bobcats and if they are hungry and weak and venture into the bobcat's wooded habitat they are easy prey.

That winter 23 of the 270 Whooping Cranes in the Aransas flock died. Unsure if they could make it to Canada because they were so weak, the Lobstick prince and his mate decided to stay in Aransas again that summer. During the summer they were barley able to find enough food to survive and the humans responsible for the cranes well being did everything they could to ensure fresh water would enter the bays and that the passes to the Gulf of Mexico stayed open. Unfortunately other humans who do not understand or care about the importance of fresh water and water from the Gulf made it hard for the cranes and the people who were trying to help them.

With all of the adversity facing the Lobstick Prince and the rest of the Aransas - Wood Buffalo Flock, he has adapted well and continues to capture the hearts of the people which gives them hope and determination to protect all of the Whooping Cranes and their last remaining habitat.